The Nose

Nikolai Gogol

translated by Claud Field

ISBN: 9798715553898

On the 25th March, 18—, a very strange occurrence took place in St Petersburg. On the Ascension Avenue there lived a barber of the name of Ivan Jakovlevitch. He had lost his family name, and on his sign-board, on which was depicted the head of a gentleman with one cheek soaped, the only inscription to be read was, "Blood-letting done here." On this particular morning, he awoke pretty early. Becoming aware of the smell of fresh-baked bread, he sat up a little in bed and saw his wife, who had a special partiality for coffee, in the act of taking some fresh-baked bread out of the oven.

"Today, Prasskovna Ossipovna," he said, "I do not want any coffee ; I should like a fresh loaf with onions."

"The blockhead may eat bread only as far as I am concerned," said his wife to herself; "then I shall have a chance of getting some coffee." And she threw a loaf on the table.

For the sake of propriety, Ivan Jakovlevitch drew a coat over his shirt, sat down at the table, shook out some salt for himself, prepared two onions assumed a serious expression and began to cut the bread. After he had cut the loaf in two halves, he looked, and to his great astonishment saw something whitish sticking in it. He carefully poked round it with his knife, and felt it with his finger.

"Quite firmly fixed !' " he murmured in his beard. " What can it be?"

He put in his finger, and drew out—a nose! Ivan Jakovlevitch at first let his hands fall from sheer astonishment; then he rubbed his eyes and began to feel it. A nose, an actual nose; and, moreover, it seemed to be the nose of an acquaintance! Alarm and terror were depicted in Ivan's face, but these feelings were slight in comparison with the disgust which took possession of his wife.

"Whose nose have you cut off, you monster ?" she screamed, her face red with anger. " You scoundrel! You tippler! I myself will report you to the police! Such a rascal! Many customers have told me that while you were shaving them, you held them so tight by the nose that they could hardly sit still."

"But Ivan Jakovlevitch was more dead than alive; he saw at once that this nose could belong to no other than to Kovaloff, a member of the Municipal Committee whom he shaved every Sunday and Wednesday.

"Stop, Prasskovna Ossipovna! I will wrap it in a piece of cloth and place it in the corner. There it may remain for the present; later on, I will take it away."

"No, not there! Shall I endure an amputated nose in my room? You understand nothing except how to strop a razor. You know nothing of the duties and obligations of a respectable man. You vagabond! You good-for-nothing! Am I to undertake all responsibility for you at the police-office? Ah, you soapsmearer! You blockhead! Take it away where you like, but don't let it stay under my eyes!

"Ivan Jakovlevitch stood there flabbergasted. He thought and thought, and knew not what he thought.

"The devil knows how that happened ! " he said, at last, scratching his head behind his ear. " Whether I came home drunk last night or not, I really don't know; but in all probability, this is a quite extraordinary occurrence, for a loaf is something baked and a nose is something different. I don't understand the matter at all." And Ivan Jakovlevitch was silent. The thought that the police might find him in unlawful possession of a nose and arrest him, robbed him of all presence of mind. Already he began to have visions of a red collar with silver braid and of a sword—and he trembled all over.

At last, he finished dressing himself, and to the accompaniment of the emphatic exhortations of his spouse, he wrapped up the nose in a cloth and issued into the street.

He intended to lose it somewhere—either at somebody's door, or in a public square, or in a narrow alley; but just then, in order to complete his bad luck, he was met by an acquaintance, who showered inquiries upon him.

"Hullo, Ivan Jakovlevitch! Whom are you going to shave so early in the morning ?" etc., so that he could find no suitable opportunity to do what he wanted. Later on, he did let the nose drop, but a sentry bore down upon him with his halberd, and said, "Look out! You have let something drop !" and Ivan Jakovlevitch was obliged to pick it up and put it in his pocket.

A feeling of despair began to take possession of him; all the more as the streets became more thronged and the merchants began to open their shops. At last he resolved to go to the Isaac Bridge, where perhaps he might succeed in throwing it into the Neva.

But my conscience is a little uneasy that I have not yet given any detailed information about Ivan Jakovlevitch, an estimable man in many ways.

Like every honest Russian tradesman, Ivan Jakovlevitch was a terrible drunkard, and although he shaved other people's faces every day, his own was always unshaved. His coat (he never wore an overcoat) was quite mottled, i.e. it had been black, but become brownish-yellow; the collar was quite shiny, and instead of the three buttons, only the threads by which they had been fastened were to be seen.

Ivan Jakovlevitch was a great cynic, and when Kovaloff, the member of the Municipal Committee, said to him, as was his custom while being shaved, "Your hands always smell, Ivan Jakovlevitch" the latter answered, "What do they smell of?" "I don't know, my friend, but they smell very strong." Ivan Jakovlevitch after taking a pinch of snuff would then, by way of reprisals, set to work to soap him on the cheek, the upper lip, behind the ears, on the chin, and everywhere.

This worthy man now stood on the Isaac Bridge. At first, he looked around him, then he leaned on the railings of the bridge, as though he wished to look down and see how many fish were swimming past, and secretly threw the nose, wrapped in a little piece of cloth, into the water. He felt as though a ton weight had been lifted off him, and laughed cheerfully. Instead, however, of going to shave any officials, he turned his steps to a building, the sign-board of which bore the legend "Teas served here," in order to have a glass of punch, when suddenly he perceived at the other end of the bridge a police inspector of the imposing exterior, with long whiskers, a three-cornered hat, and a sword hanging at his side. He nearly fainted, but the police inspector beckoned to him with his hand and said, "Come here, my dear sir."

Ivan Jakovlevitch, knowing how a gentleman should behave, took his hat off quickly, went towards the police inspector and said, "I hope you are in the best of health."

"Never mind my health. Tell me, my friend, why you were standing on the bridge."

"By heaven, gracious sir, I was on the way to my customers, and only looked down to see if the river was flowing quickly."

"That is a lie! You won't get out of it like that. Confess the truth."

"I am willing to shave Your Grace two or even three times a week gratis," answered Ivan Jakovlevitch.

"No, my friend, don't put yourself out! Three barbers are busy with me already and reckon it a high honor that I let them show me their skill. Now then, out with it! What were you doing there ?"

Ivan Jakovlevitch grew pale. But here the strange episode vanishes in the mist, and what further happened is not known.

Kovaloff, the member of the Municipal Committee, awoke fairly early that morning, and made a droning noise—" Brr ! Brr ! "—through his lips, as he always did, though he could not say why. He stretched himself, and told his valet to give him a little mirror which was on the table. He wished to look at the heat-boil which had appeared on his nose the previous evening; but to his great astonishment, he saw that instead of his nose he had a perfectly smooth vacancy in his face. Thoroughly alarmed, he ordered some water to be brought, and rubbed his eyes with a towel. Sure enough, he had no longer a nose! Then he sprang out of bed, and shook himself violently ! No, no nose any more ! He dressed himself and went at once to the police superintendent.

But before proceeding further, we must certainly give the reader some information about Kovaloff, so that he may know what sort of a man this member of the Municipal Committee really was. These committee-men, who obtain that title by means of certificates of learning, must not be compared with the committee-men appointed for the Caucasus district, who are of quite a different kind. The learned committee man—but Russia is such a wonderful country that when one committee-man is spoken of all the others from Eiga to Kamschatka refer it to themselves. The same is also true of all other titled officials. Kovaloff had been a Caucasian committee-man two years previously, and could not forget that he had occupied that position; but in order to enhance his own importance, he never called himself "committee-man" but "Major."

"Listen, my dear," he used to say when he met an old woman in the street who sold shirtfronts; "go to my house in Sadovaia Street and ask 'Does Major Kovaloff live here?' Any child can tell you where it is."

Accordingly we will call him for the future Major Kovaloff. It was his custom to take a daily walk on the Neffsky Avenue. The collar of his shirt was always remarkably clean and stiff. He wore the same style of whiskers as those that are worn by governors of districts, architects, and regimental doctors ; in short, all those who have full red cheeks and play a good game of whist. These whiskers grow straight across the cheek towards the nose.

Major Kovaloff wore a number of seals, on some of which were engraved armorial bearings, and others the names of the days of the week. He had come to St Petersburg with the view of obtaining some position corresponding to his rank, if possible that of vice-governor of a province ; but he was prepared to be content with that of a bailiff in some department or other. He was, moreover, not disinclined to marry, but only such a lady who could bring with her a dowry of two hundred thousand roubles. Accordingly, the reader can judge for himself what his sensations were when he found in his face, instead of a fairly symmetrical nose, a broad, flat vacancy.

To increase his misfortune, not a single droshky was to be seen in the street, and so he was obliged to proceed on foot. He wrapped himself up in his cloak, and held his handkerchief to his face as though his nose bled. "But perhaps it is all only my imagination ; it is impossible that a nose should drop off in such a silly way," he thought, and stepped into a confectioner's shop in order to look into the mirror.

Fortunately no customer was in the shop; only small shop-boys were cleaning it out, and putting chairs and tables straight. Others with sleepy faces were carrying fresh cakes on trays, and yesterday's newspapers stained with coffee were still lying about. "Thank God no one is here!" he said to himself. "Now I can look at myself leisurely."

He stepped gingerly up to a mirror and looked.

" What an infernal face !" he exclaimed, and spat with disgust. "If there were only something there instead of the nose, but there is absolutely nothing."

He bit his lips with vexation, left the confectioner's, and resolved, quite contrary to his habit, neither to look nor smile at anyone on the street. Suddenly he halted as if rooted to the spot before a door, where something extraordinary happened. A carriage drew up at the entrance ; the carriage door was opened, and a gentleman in uniform came out and hurried up the steps. How great was Kovaloff's terror and astonishment when he saw that it was his own nose !

At this extraordinary sight, everything seemed to turn round with him. He felt as though he could hardly keep upright on his legs; but, though trembling all over as though with fever, he resolved to wait till the nose should return to the carriage. After about two minutes the nose actually came out again. It wore a gold-embroidered uniform with a stiff, high collar, trousers of chamois leather, and a sword hung at its side. The hat, adorned with a plume, showed that it held the rank of a state-councillor. It was obvious that it was paying "duty-calls." It looked round on both sides, called to the coachman "Drive on," and got into the carriage, which drove away.

Poor Kovaloff nearly lost his reason. He did not know what to think of this extraordinary procedure. And indeed how was it possible that the nose, which only yesterday he had on his face, and which could neither walk nor drive, should wear a uniform. He ran after the carriage, which fortunately had stopped a short way off before the Grand Bazar of Moscow. He hurried towards it and pressed through a crowd of beggar-women with their faces bound up, leaving only two openings for the eyes, over whom he had formerly so often made merry.

There were only a few people in front of the Bazar. Kovaloff was so agitated that he could decide on nothing, and looked for the nose everywhere. At last he saw it standing before a shop. It seemed half buried in its stiff collar, and was attentively inspecting the wares displayed.

"How can I get at it?" thought Kovaloff. "Everything—the uniform, the hat, and so on —show that it is a state-councillor. How the deuce has that happened?"

He began to cough discreetly near it, but the nose paid him not the least attention. "Honourable sir," said Kovaloff at last, plucking up courage, "honourable sir."

" What do you want?" asked the nose, and turned round.

"It seems to me strange, most respected sir-—you should know where you belong—and I find you all of a sudden—where? Judge yourself."

"Pardon me, I do not understand what you are talking about. Explain yourself more distinctly."

How shall I make my meaning plainer to him?" Then plucking up fresh courage, he continued, "Naturally—besides I am a Major. You must admit it is not befitting that I should go about without a nose. An old apple-woman on the Ascension Bridge may carry on her business without one, but since I am on the look out for a post; besides in many houses I am acquainted with ladies of high position—Madame Tchektyriev, wife of a state-councillor, and many others. So you see—I do not know, honourable sir, what you—(here the Major shrugged his shoulders). "Pardon me; if one regards the matter from the point of view of duty and honour—you will yourself understand—"

"I understand nothing," answered the nose. "I repeat, please explain yourself more distinctly."

"Honourable sir," said Kovaloff with dignity, "I do not know how I am to understand your words. It seems to me the matter is as clear as possible. Or do you wish—but you are after all my own nose !

The nose looked at the Major and wrinkled its forehead. "There you are wrong, respected sir; I am myself. Besides, there can be no close relations between us. To judge by the buttons of your uniform, you must be in quite a different department to mine." So saying, the nose turned away.

Kovaloff was completely puzzled; he did not know what to do, and still less what to think. At this moment he heard the pleasant rustling of a lady's dress, and there approached an elderly lady wearing a quantity of lace, and by her side her graceful daughter in a white dress which set off her slender figure to advantage, and wearing a light straw hat. Behind the ladies marched a tall lackey with long whiskers.

Kovaloff advanced a few steps, adjusted his cambric collar, arranged his seals which hung by a little gold chain, and with smiling face fixed his eyes on the graceful lady, who bowed lightly like a spring flower, and raised to her brow her little white hand with transparent fingers. He smiled still more when he spied under the brim of her hat her little round chin, and part of her cheek faintly tinted with rose-colour. But suddenly he sprang back as though he had been scorched. He remembered that he had nothing but an absolute blank in place of a nose, and tears started to his eyes. He turned round in order to tell the gentleman in uniform that he was only a state-councillor in appearance, but really a scoundrel and a rascal, and nothing else but his own nose; but the nose was no longer there. He had had time to go, doubtless in order to continue his visits.

His disappearance plunged Kovaloff into despair. He went back and stood for a moment under a colonnade, looking round him on all sides in hope of perceiving the nose somewhere. He remembered very well that it wore a hat with a plume in it and a gold-embroidered uniform; but he had not noticed the shape of the cloak, nor the colour of the carriages and the horses, nor even whether a lackey stood behind it, and, if so, what sort of livery he wore. Moreover, so many carriages were passing that it would have been difficult to recognise one, and even if he had done so, there would have been no means of stopping it.

The day was fine and sunny. An immense crowd was passing to and fro in the Neffsky Avenue; a variegated stream of ladies flowed along the pavement. There was his acquaintance, the Privy Councillor, whom he was accustomed to style "General," especially when strangers were present. There was Iarygin, his intimate friend who always lost in the evenings at whist; and there another Major, who had obtained the rank of committee-man in the Caucasus, beckoned to him.

"Go to the deuce !" said Kovaloff sotto voce. '' Hi ! coachman, drive me straight to the superintendent of police." So saying, he got into a droshky and continued to shout all the time to the coachman "Drive hard! "

"Is the police superintendent at home?" he asked on entering the front hall.

"No, sir," answered the porter," he has just gone out."

"Ah, just as I thought!"

"Yes," continued the porter, "he has only just gone out; if you had been a moment earlier you would perhaps have caught him."

Kovaloff, still holding his handkerchief to his face, re-entered the droshky and cried in a despairing voice "Drive on !

""Where?" asked the coachman.

"Straight on!"

"But how? There are cross-roads here. Shall I go to the right or the left?"

This question made Kovaloff: reflect. In his situation it was necessary to have recourse to the police ; not because the affair had anything to do with them directly but because they acted more promptly than other authorities. As for demanding any explanation from the department to which the nose claimed to belong, it would, he felt, be useless, for the answers of that gentleman showed that he regarded nothing as sacred, and he might just as likely have lied in this matter as in saying that he had never seen Kovaloff.

But just as he was about to order the coachman to drive to the police-station, the idea occurred to him that this rascally scoundrel who, at their first meeting, had behaved so disloyally towards him, might, profiting by the delay, quit the city secretly ; and then all his searching would be in vain, or might last over a whole month. Finally, as though visited with a heavenly inspiration, he resolved to go directly to an advertisement office, and to advertise the loss of his nose, giving all its distinctive characteristics in detail, so that anyone who found it might bring it at once to him, or at any rate inform him where it lived. Having decided on this course, he ordered the coachman to drive to the advertisement office, and all the way he continued to punch him in the back— "Quick, scoundrel ! quick !"

"Yes, sir !" answered the coachman, lashing his shaggy horse with the reins.

At last they arrived, and Kovaloff, out of breath, rushed into a little room where a grey haired official, in an old coat and with spectacles on his nose, sat at a table holding his pen between his teeth, counting a heap of copper coins.

"Who takes in the advertisements here?" exclaimed Kovaloff.

"At your service, sir," answered the grey haired functionary, looking up and then fastening his eyes again on the heap of coins before him.

"I wish to place an advertisement in your paper—"

"Have the kindness to wait a minute," answered the official, putting down figures on paper with one hand, and with the other moving two balls on his calculating-frame.

A lackey, whose silver-laced coat showed that he served in one of the houses of the nobility, was standing by the table with a note in his hand, and speaking in a lively tone, by way of showing himself sociable. " Would you believe it, sir, this little dog is really not worth twenty-four kopecks, and for my own part I would not give a farthing for it; but the countess is quite gone upon it, and offers a hundred roubles' reward to anyone who finds it. To tell you the truth, the tastes of these people are very different from ours; they don't mind giving five hundred or a thousand roubles for a poodle or a pointer, provided it be a good one."

The official listened with a serious air while counting the number of letters contained in the note. At either side of the table stood a number of housekeepers, clerks and porters, carrying notes. The writer of one wished to sell a barouche, which had been brought from Paris in 1814 and had been very little used; others wanted to dispose of a strong droshky which wanted one spring, a spirited horse seventeen years old, and so on. The room where these people were collected was very small, and the air was very close ; but Kovaloff was not affected by it, for he had covered his face with a handkerchief, and because his nose itself was heaven knew where.

"Sir, allow me to ask you—I am in a great hurry," he said at last impatiently.

"In a moment ! In a moment ! Two roubles, twenty-four kopecks—one minute ! One rouble, sixty-four kopecks !" said the grey-haired official, throwing their notes back to the housekeepers and porters. " What do you wish?" he said, turning to Kovaloff.

"I wish—" answered the latter, "I have just been swindled and cheated, and I cannot get hold of the perpetrator. I only want you to insert an advertisement to say that whoever brings this scoundrel to me will be well rewarded."

" What is your name, please?

"Why do you want my name? I have many lady friends— Madame Tchektyriev, wife of a state-councillor, Madame Podtotchina, wife of a Colonel. Heaven forbid that they should get to hear of it. You can simply write 'committeeman' or, better, 'Major.'"

"And the man who has run away is your serf."

"Serf! If he was, it would not be such a great swindle! It is the nose which has absconded."

"H'm! What a strange name. And this Mr Nose has stolen from you a considerable sum?"

"Mr Nose! Ah, you don't understand me! It is my own nose which has gone, I don't know where. The devil has played a trick on me."

"How has it disappeared? I don't understand."

"I can't tell you how, but the important point is that now it walks about the city itself a state councillor. That is why I want you to advertise that whoever gets hold of it should bring it as soon as possible to me. Consider; how can I live without such a prominent part of my body? It is not as if it were merely a little toe ; I would only have to put my foot in my boot and no one would notice its absence. Every Thursday I call on the wife of M. Tchektyriev, the state councillor; Madame Podtotchina, a Colonel's wife who has a very pretty daughter, is one of my acquaintances; and what am I to do now? I cannot appear before them like this."

The official compressed his lips and reflected. "No, I cannot insert an advertisement like that," he said after a long pause.

"What! Why not?"

"Because it might compromise the paper. Suppose everyone could advertise that his nose was lost. People already say that all sorts of nonsense and lies are inserted."

"But this is not nonsense ! There is nothing of that sort in my case."

"You think so? Listen a minute. Last week there was a case very like it. An official came, just as you have done, bringing an advertisement for the insertion of which he paid two roubles, sixty-three kopecks; and this advertisement simply announced the loss of a black-haired poodle. There did not seem to be anything out of the way in it, but it was really a satire ; by the poodle was meant the cashier of some establishment or other."

"But I am not talking of a poodle, but my own nose; i.e. almost myself."

"No, I cannot insert your advertisement."

"But my nose really has disappeared!"

"That is a matter for a doctor. There are said to be people who can provide you with any kind of nose you like. But I see that you are a witty man, and like to have your little joke."

"But I swear to you on my word of honour. Look at my face yourself."

"Why put yourself out?" continued the official, taking a pinch of snuff." All the same, if you don't mind," he added with a touch of curiosity, "I should like to have a look at it."

The committee-man removed the handkerchief from before his face.

"It certainly does look odd," said the official. "It is perfectly flat like a freshly fried pancake. It is hardly credible."

"Very well. Are you going to hesitate any more? You see it is impossible to refuse to advertise my loss. I shall be particularly obliged to you, and I shall be glad that this incident has procured me the pleasure of making your acquaintance."

The Major, we see, did not even shrink from a slight humiliation.

"It certainly is not difficult to advertise it," replied the official;" but I don't see what good it would do you. However, if you lay so much stress on it, you should apply to someone who has a skilful pen, so that he may describe it as a curious, natural freak, and publish the article in the Northern Bee" (here he took another pinch) "for the benefit of youthful readers (he wiped his nose), "or simply as a matter worthy of arousing public curiosity."

The committee-man felt completely discouraged. He let his eyes fall absent-mindedly on a daily paper in which theatrical performances were advertised. Eeading there the name of an actress whom he knew to be pretty, he involuntarily smiled, and his hand sought his pocket to see if he had a blue ticket— for in Kovaloffs opinion superior officers like himself should not take a lesser-priced seat; but the thought of his lost nose suddenly spoilt everything.

The official himself seemed touched at his difficult position. Desiring to console him, he tried to express his sympathy by a few polite words. "I much regret," he said, "your extraordinary mishap. Will you not try a pinch of snuff? It clears the head, banishes depression, and is a good preventive against haemorroids."

So saying, he reached his snuff-box out to Kovaloff, skilfully concealing at the same time the cover, which was adorned with the portrait of some lady or other.

This act, quite innocent in itself, exasperated Kovaloff. "I don't understand what you find to joke about in the matter," he exclaimed angrily. "Don't you see that I lack precisely the essential feature for taking snuff? The devil take your snuff-box. I don't want to look at snuff now, not even the best, certainly not your vile stuff!"

So saying, he left the advertisement office in a state of profound irritation, and went to the commissary of police. He arrived just as this dignitary was reclining on his couch, and saying to himself with a sigh of satisfaction, "Yes, I shall make a nice little sum out of that."

It might be expected, therefore, that the committee-man's visit would be quite inopportune. This police commissary was a great patron of all the arts and industries; but what he liked above everything else was a cheque. "It is a thing," he used to say, "to which it is not easy to find an equivalent ; it requires no food, it does not take up much room, it stays in one's pocket, and if it falls, it is not broken."

The commissary accorded Kovaloff a fairly frigid reception, saying that the afternoon was not the best time to come with a case, that nature required one to rest a little after eating (this showed the committee-man that the commissary was acquainted with the aphorisms of the ancient sages), and that respectable people did not have their noses stolen.

The last allusion was too direct. We must remember that Kovaloff was a very sensitive man. He did not mind anything said against him as an individual, but he could not endure any reflection on his rank or social position. He even believed that in comedies one might allow attacks on junior officers, but never on their seniors.

The commissary's reception of him hurt his feelings so much that he raised his head proudly, and said with dignity, "After such insulting expressions on your part, I have nothing more to say." And he left the place.

He reached his house quite wearied out. It was already growing dark. After all his fruitless search, his room seemed to him melancholy and even ugly. In the vestibule he saw his valet Ivan stretched on the leather couch and amusing himself by spitting at the ceiling, which he did very cleverly, hitting every time the same spot. His servant's equanimity enraged him; he struck him on the forehead with his hat, and said, "You good-for-nothing, you are always playing the fool!"

Ivan rose quickly and hastened to take off his master's cloak.

Once in his room, the Major, tired and depressed, threw himself in an armchair and, after sighing a while, began to soliloquise : "In heaven's name, why should such a misfortune befall me? If I had lost an arm or a leg, it would be less insupportable; but a man without a nose ! Devil take it !—what is he good for? He is only fit to be thrown out of the window. If it had been taken from me in war or in a duel, or if I had lost it by my own fault! But it has disappeared inexplicably. But no ! it is impossible," he continued after reflecting a few moments, "it is incredible that a nose can disappear like that—quite incredible. I must be dreaming, or suffering from some hallucination ; perhaps I swallowed, by mistake instead of water, the brandy with which I rub my chin after being shaved. That fool of an Ivan must have forgotten to take it away, and I must have swallowed it."

In order to find out whether he were really drunk, the Major pinched himself so hard that he unvoluntarily uttered a cry. The pain convinced him that he was quite wide awake. He walked slowly to the looking-glass and at first closed his eyes, hoping to see his nose suddenly in its proper place; but on opening them, he started back. "What a hideous sight!" he exclaimed.

It was really incomprehensible. One might easily lose a button, a silver spoon, a watch, or something similar; but a loss like this, and in one's own dwelling !

After considering all the circumstances, Major Kovaloff felt inclined to suppose that the cause of all his trouble should be laid at the door of Madame Podtotchina, the Colonel's wife, who wished him to marry her daughter. He himself paid her court readily, but always avoided coming to the point. And when the lady one day told him point-blank that she wished him to marry her daughter, he gently drew back, declaring that he was still too young, and that he had to serve five years more before he would be forty-two. This must be the reason why the lady, in revenge, had resolved to bring him into disgrace, and had hired two sorceresses for that object. One thing was certain—his nose had not been cut off; no one had entered his room, and as for Ivan Jakovlevitch—he had been shaved by him on Wednesday, and during that day and the whole of Thursday his nose had been there, as he knew and well remembered. Moreover, if his nose had been cut off he would naturally have felt pain, and doubtless the wound would not have healed so quickly, nor would the surface have been as flat as a pancake.

All kinds of plans passed through his head : should he bring a legal action against the wife of a superior officer, or should he go to her and charge her openly with her treachery?

His reflections were interrupted by a sudden light, which shone through all the chinks of the door, showing that Ivan had lit the wax-candles in the vestibule. Soon Ivan himself came in with the lights. Kovaloff quickly seized a handkerchief and covered the place where his nose had been the evening before, so that his blockhead of a servant might not gape with his mouth wide open when he saw his master's extraordinary appearance.

Scarcely had Ivan returned to the vestibule than a stranger's voice was heard there.

"Does Major Kovaloff live here?" it asked.

"Come in!" said the Major, rising rapidly and opening the door.

He saw a police official of pleasant appearance, with grey whiskers and fairly full cheeks—the same who at the commencement of this story was standing at the end of the Isaac Bridge. "Have you lost your nose?" he asked.

"Exactly so.'

"It has just been found."

"What are you saying?" stammered Major Kovaloff.

Joy had suddenly paralysed his tongue. He stared at the police commissary on whose cheeks and full lips fell the flickering light of the candle.

"How was it?" he asked at last.

"By a very singular chance. It has been arrested just as it was getting into a carriage for Eiga. Its passport had been made out some time ago in the name of an official ; and what is still more strange, I myself took it at first for a gentleman. Fortunately I had my glasses with me, and then I saw at once that it was a nose. I am shortsighted, you know, and as you stand before me I cannot distinguish your nose, your beard, or anything else. My mother-in-law can hardly see at all."

Kovaloff was beside himself with excitement. "Where is it? Where? I will hasten there at once."

"Don't put yourself out. Knowing that you need it, I have brought it with me. Another singular thing is that the principal culprit in the matter is a scoundrel of a barber living in the Ascension Avenue, who is now safely locked up. I had long suspected him of drunkenness and theft; only the day before yesterday he stole some buttons in a shop. Your nose is quite uninjured." So saying, the police commissary put his hand in his pocket and brought out the nose wrapped up in paper.

"Yes, yes, that is it!" exclaimed Kovaloff. "Will you not stay and drink a cup of tea with me?"

"I should like to very much, but I cannot. I must go at once to the House of Correction. The cost of living is very high nowadays. My mother-in-law lives with me, and there are several children; the eldest is very hopeful and intelligent, but I have no means for their education."

After the commissary's departure, Kovaloff remained for some time plunged in a kind of vague reverie, and did not recover full consciousness for several moments, so great was the effect of this unexpected good news. He placed the recovered nose carefully in the palm of his hand, and examined it again with the greatest attention.

"Yes, this is it !" he said to himself. "Here is the heat-boil on the left side, which came out yesterday." And he nearly laughed aloud with delight.

But nothing is permanent in this world. Joy in the second moment of its arrival is already less keen than in the first, is still fainter in the third, and finishes by coalescing with our normal mental state, just as the circles which the fall of a pebble forms on the surface of water, gradually die away. Kovaloff began to meditate, and saw that his difficulties were not yet over; his nose had been recovered, but it had to be joined on again in its proper place.

And suppose it could not? As he put this question to himself, Kovaloff grew pale. With a feeling of indescribable dread, he rushed towards his dressing-table, and stood before the mirror in order that he might not place his nose crookedly. His hands trembled.

Very carefully he placed it where it had been before. Horror! It did not remain there. He held it to his mouth and warmed it a little with his breath, and then placed it there again; but it would not hold.

"Hold on, you stupid!" he said.

But the nose seemed to be made of wood, and fell back on the table with a strange noise, as though it had been a cork. The Major's face began to twitch feverishly. "Is it possible that it won't stick?" he asked himself, full of alarm. But however often he tried, all his efforts were in vain.

He called Ivan, and sent him to fetch the doctor who occupied the finest flat in the mansion. This doctor was a man of imposing appearance, who had magnificent black whiskers and a healthy wife. He ate fresh apples every morning, and cleaned his teeth with extreme care, using five different toothbrushes for three-quarters of an hour daily.

The doctor came immediately. After having asked the Major when this misfortune had happened, he raised his chin and gave him a fillip with his finger just where the nose had been, in such a way that the Major suddenly threw back his head and struck the wall with it. The doctor said that did not matter; then, making him turn his face to the right, he felt the vacant place and said " H'm! " then he made him turn it to the left and did the same ; finally he again gave him a fillip with his finger, so that the Major started like a horse whose teeth are being examined. After this experiment, the doctor shook his head and said, "No, it cannot be done. Either remain as you are, lest something worse happen. Certainly one could replace it at once, but I assure you the remedy would be worse than the disease."

"All very fine, but how am I to go on without a nose?" answered Kovaloff. "There is nothing worse than that. How can I show myself with such a villainous appearance ? I go into good society, and this evening I am invited to two parties. I know several ladies, Madame Tchektyriev, the wife of a state-councillor, Madame Podtotchina—although after what she has done, I don't want to have anything to do with her except through the agency of the police. I beg you," continued Kovaloff in a supplicating tone, "find some way or other of replacing it; even if it is not quite firm, as long as it holds at all; I can keep it in place sometimes with my hand, whenever there is any risk. Besides, I do not even dance, so that it is not likely to be injured by any sudden movement. As to your fee, be in no anxiety about that; I can well afford it."

"Believe me," answered the doctor in a voice which was neither too high nor too low, but soft and almost magnetic, "I do not treat patients from love of gain. That would be contrary to my principles and to my art. It is true that I accept fees, but that is only not to hurt my patients' feelings by refusing them. I could certainly replace your nose, but I assure you on my word of honour, it would only make matters worse. Bather let Nature do her own work. Wash the place often with cold water, and I assure you that even without a nose, you will be just as well as if you had one. As to the nose itself, I advise you to have it preserved in a bottle of spirits, or, still better, of warm vinegar mixed with two spoonfuls of brandy, and then you can sell it at a good price. I would be willing to take it myself, provided you do not ask too much."

"No, no, I shall not sell it at any price. I would rather it were lost again."

"Excuse me," said the doctor, taking his leave. "I hoped to be useful to you, but I can do nothing more ; you are at any rate convinced of my good-will." So saying, the doctor left the room with a dignified air.

Kovaloff did not even notice his departure. Absorbed in a profound reverie, he only saw the edge of his snow-white cuffs emerging from the sleeves of his black coat.

The next day he resolved, before bringing a formal action, to write to the Colonel's wife and see whether she would not return to him, without further dispute, that of which she had deprived him.

The letter ran as follows :

To Madame Alexandra Podtotchina,

"I hardly understand your method of action. Be sure that by adopting such a course you will gain nothing, and will certainly not succeed in making me marry your daughter. Believe me, the story of my nose has become well known; it is you and no one else who have taken the principal part in it. Its unexpected separation from the place which it occupied, its flight and its appearances sometimes in the disguise of an official, sometimes in proper person, are nothing but the consequence of unholy spells employed by you or by persons who, like you, are addicted to such honourable pursuits. On my part, I wish to inform you, that if the above-mentioned nose is not restored to-day to its proper place, I shall be obliged to have recourse to legal procedure. "For the rest, with all respect, I have the honour to be your humble servant,

"Platon Kovaloff."

The reply was not long in coming, and was as follows :

"Major Platon Kovaloff,—

"Your letter has profoundly astonished me. I must confess that I had not expected such unjust reproaches on your part. I assure you that the official of whom you speak has not been at my house, either disguised or in his proper person. It is true that Philippe Ivanovitch Potantchikoff has paid visits at my house, and though he Has actually asked for my daughter's hand, and was a man of good breeding, respectable and intelligent, I never gave him any hope. " Again, you say something about a nose. If you intend to imply by that that I wished to snub you, i.e. to meet you with a refusal, I am very astonished because, as you well know, I was quite of the opposite mind. If after this you wish to ask for my daughter's hand, I should be glad to gratify you, for such has also been the object of my most fervent desire, in the hope of the accomplishment of which, I remain, yours most sincerely,

"Alexandra Podtotchina."

"No," said Kovaloff, after having reperused the letter, "she is certainly not guilty. It is impossible. Such a letter could not be written by a criminal." The committee-man was experienced in such matters, for he had been often officially deputed to conduct criminal investigations while in the Caucasus. "But then how and by what trick of fate has the thing happened?" he said to himself with a gesture of discouragement. "The devil must be at the bottom of it."

Meanwhile the rumour of this extraordinary event had spread all over the city, and, as is generally the case, not without numerous additions. At that period there was a general disposition to believe in the miraculous; the public had recently been impressed by experiments in magnetism. The story of the floating chairs in Koniouchennaia Street was still quite recent, and there was nothing astonishing in hearing soon afterwards that Major Kovaloffs nose was to be seen walking every day at three o'clock on the Neffsky Avenue. The crowd of curious spectators which gathered there daily was enormous. On one occasion someone spread a report that the nose was in Junker's stores and immediately the place was besieged by such a crowd that the police had to interfere and establish order. A certain speculator with a grave, whiskered face, who sold cakes at a theatre door, had some strong wooden benches made which he placed before the window of the stores, and obligingly invited the public to stand on them and look in, at the modest charge of twenty-four kopecks. A veteran colonel, leaving his house earlier than usual expressly for the purpose, had the greatest difficulty in elbowing his way through the crowd, but to his great indignation he saw nothing in the store window but an ordinary flannel waistcoat and a coloured lithograph representing a young girl darning a stocking, while an elegant youth in a waistcoat with large lappels watched her from behind a tree. The picture had hung in the same place for more than ten years. The colonel went off, growling savagely to himself: How can the fools let themselves be excited by such idiotic stories?"

Then another rumour got abroad, to the effect that the nose of Major Kovaloff was in the habit of walking not on the Neffsky Avenue but in the Tauris Gardens. Some students of the Academy of Surgery went there on purpose to see it. A high-born lady wrote to the keeper of the gardens asking him to show her children this rare phenomenon, and to give them some suitable instruction on the occasion.

All these incidents were eagerly collected by the town wits, who just then were very short of anecdotes adapted to amuse ladies. On the other hand, the minority of solid, sober people were very much displeased. One gentleman asserted with great indignation that he could not understand how in our enlightened age such absurdities could spread abroad, and he was astonished that the Government did not direct their attention to the matter. This gentleman evidently belonged to the category of those people who wish the Government to interfere in everything, even in their daily quarrels with their wives.

But here the course of events is again obscured by a veil.

❦❦❦

Strange events happen in this world, events which are sometimes entirely improbable. The same nose which had masqueraded as a state-councilor, and caused so much sensation in the town, was found one morning in its proper place, i.e. between the cheeks of Major Kovaloff, as if nothing had happened.

This occurred on 7th April. On awaking, the Major looked by chance into a mirror and percieved a nose. He quickly put his hand to it; it was there beyond a doubt!

"Oh!" exclaimed Kovaloff. For sheer joy he was on the point of performing a dance barefooted across his room, but the entrance of Ivan prevented him. He told him to bring water, and after washing himself, he looked again in the glass. The nose was there ! Then he dried his face with a towel and looked again. Yes, there was no mistake about it !

"Look here, Ivan, it seems to me that I have a heat-boil on my nose," he said to his valet.

And he thought to himself at the same time, "That will be a nice business if Ivan says to me 'No, sir, not only is there no boil, but your nose itself is not there !'"

But Ivan answered, "There is nothing, sir ; I can see no boil on your nose."

"Good! Good!" exclaimed the Major, and snapped his fingers with delight.

At this moment the barber, Ivan Jakovlevitch, put his head in at the door, but as timidly as a cat which has just been beaten for stealing lard.

"Tell me first, are your hands clean?" asked Kovaloff when he saw him.

"Yes, sir."

"You lie."

"I swear they are perfectly clean, sir."

"Very well; then come here."

Kovaloff seated himself. Jakovlevitch tied a napkin under his chin, and in the twinkling of an eye covered his beard and part of his cheeks with a copious creamy lather.

"There it is!" said the barber to himself, as he glanced at the nose. Then he bent his head a little and examined it from one side. "Yes, it actually is the nose—really, when one thinks—" he continued, pursuing his mental soliloquy and still looking at it. Then quite gently, with infinite precaution, he raised two fingers in the air in order to take hold of it by the extremity, as he was accustomed to do.

" Now then, take care!" Kovaloff exclaimed.

Ivan Jakovlevitch let his arm fall and felt more embarrassed than he had ever done in his life. At last he began to pass the razor very lightly over the Major's chin, and although it was very difficult to shave him without using the olfactory organ as a point of support, he succeeded, however, by placing his wrinkled thumb against the Major's lower jaw and cheek, thus overcoming all obstacles and bringing his task to a safe conclusion.

When the barber had finished, Kovaloff hastened to dress himself, took a droshky, and drove straight to the confectioner's. As he entered it, he ordered a cup of chocolate. He then stepped straight to the mirror ; the nose was there !

He returned joyfully, and regarded with a satirical expression two officers who were in the shop, one of whom possessed a nose not much larger than a waistcoat button. After that he went to the office of the department where he had applied for the post of vice-governor of a province or Government bailiff. As he passed through the hall of reception, he cast a glance at the mirror ; the nose was there ! Then he went to pay a visit to another committeeman, a very sarcastic personage, to whom he was a"ccustomed to say in answer to his raillery, Yes, I know, you are the funniest fellow in St Petersburg."

On the way he said to himself, "If the Major does not burst into laughter at the sight of me, that is a most certain sign that everything is in its accustomed place."

But the Major said nothing.

"Very good !" thought Kovaloff.

As he returned, he met Madame Podtotchina with her daughter. He accosted them, and they responded very graciously. The conversation lasted a long time, during which he took more than one pinch of snuff, saying to himself, "No, you haven't caught me yet, coquettes that you are ! And as to the daughter, I shan't marry her at all."

After that, the Major resumed his walks on the Neffsky Avenue and his visits to the theatre as if nothing had happened. His nose also remained in its place as if it had never quitted it. From that time he was always to be seen smiling, in a good humour, and paying attentions to pretty girls.

Such was the occurrence which took place in the northern capital of our vast empire. On considering the account carefully we see that there is a good deal which looks improbable about it. Not to speak of the strange disappearance of the nose, and its appearance in different places under the disguise of a councillor of state, how was it that Kovaloff did not understand that one cannot decently advertise for a lost nose? I do not mean to say that he would have had to pay too much for the advertisement—that is a mere trifle, and I am not one of those who attach too much importance to money; but to advertise in Such a case is not proper nor befitting.

Another difficulty is—how was the nose found in the baked loaf, and how did Ivan Jakovlevitch himself—no, I don't understand it at all !

But the most incomprehensible thing of all is, how authors can choose such subjects for their stories. That really surpasses my understanding. In the first place, no advantage results from it for the country; and in the second place, no harm results either.

All the same, when one reflects well, there really is something in the matter. Whatever may be said to the contrary, such cases do occur—rarely, it is true, but now and then actually.

Table of contents

I. 3

II. 9

III. 39

IV 44

Printed in Great Britain
by Amazon